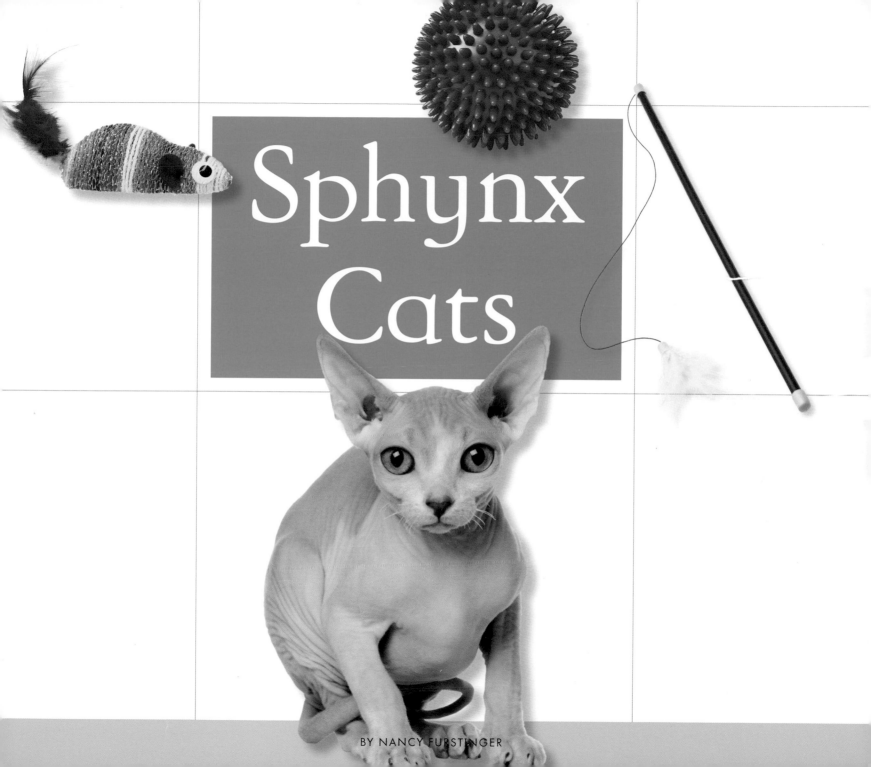

Sphynx Cats

BY NANCY FURSTINGER

Published by The Child's World®
1980 Lookout Drive • Mankato, MN 56003-1705
800-599-READ • www.childsworld.com

Acknowledgments
The Child's World®: Mary Berendes, Publishing Director
Red Line Editorial: Editorial direction
The Design Lab: Design
Amnet: Production
Design elements: iStockphoto; Ivonne Wierink/Shutterstock
Images; Shutterstock Images; Willem Havenaar/Shutterstock
Images

Photographs ©: iStockphoto, cover, 1, 12, 23; Ivonne
Wierink/Shutterstock Images, cover, 1; Shutterstock Images,
cover, 1; Willem Havenaar/Shutterstock Images, cover, 1;
Anna Nemkovich/Shutterstock Images, 4; Vladimir Sorokin/
iStockphoto, 7; Jarda Schuler/Shutterstock Images, 9; Yuryi
Oleinikov/Shutterstock Images, 11; Chad Zuber/Shutterstock
Images, 15; Bureau L.A. Collection/Sygma/Corbis, 17;
Loginova Elena/Shutterstock Images, 18; Marisha Sha/
Shutterstock Images, 21

ISBN 9781626873889
LCCN 2014930644

Printed in the United States of America
Mankato, MN
July, 2014
PA02226

ABOUT THE AUTHOR

Nancy Furstinger has been speaking up for animals since she learned to talk. She is the author of nearly 100 books, including many on her favorite topic: animals! She shares her home with big dogs and house rabbits.

CONTENTS

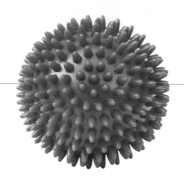

Tame Wild Cats

The Sphynx cat is an unusual cat breed. People have to look twice when they see this cat for the first time. Sphynx cats are bald and wrinkly. Some people like the Sphynx because of its special looks. Other people enjoy the cat's friendly personality.

The Sphynx is powerfully built. It has muscles like its bigger wild cousin, the tiger. It also has plenty of energy. The Sphynx will pounce on **prey** the same way a wild cat would.

Today there are 600 million house cats around the world. Cats in the United States belong to one of 42 different breeds. The Sphynx is one of these breeds. These cats have many nicknames. Some people call them the birthday suit cats. Others call these cats by their French name, *Chat sans Poils*. This means "the naked cat."

Sphynx cats love playing with children. This breed doesn't like to be left alone. Some people get their Sphynx another pet pal, such as a cat or dog. This helps keep them company!

Sphynx cats look different than most other cat breeds since they are hairless.

Bald Kitties

Hairless cats have appeared in litters around the world for more than 100 years. Bald kittens were born to parents who had fur.

Native Americans gave away a pair of hairless cats in New Mexico in the early 1900s. The breed was called the Mexican hairless cat. This was the first recorded hairless cat breed.

A cat in Canada gave birth to a hairless kitten in 1966. The owner named the kitten Prune. Prune was later bred to other cats. Some of the kittens looked just like Prune. This breed was called the Canadian hairless cat. They had many health problems. People stopped breeding these cats.

Hairless cats fascinated breeders. These cats are considered mutations. This means something changes and a new form is created. Other mutations include cats with extra toes and cats with folded ears. These changes happen by accident. These cats can then be bred for their special looks.

Hairless cats were rare. People prized this uncommon breed. They wanted to continue breeding these one-of-a-kind cats.

Hairless Sphynx cats were born by chance.

Sphynx cats are named after a pretend creature found in Egyptian myths. The sphinx has the body of a lion and the head of a human.

Rare Treasures

The first Sphynx cats were bred to cats with fur. Two breeds that were used were the Devon Rex and the American shorthair. The Devon Rex has a short coat and huge ears. The American shorthair has a short, thick coat and a powerful body. This mix of other cat breeds helped make sure the kittens would be healthy. However, only kittens with fur were born in those litters.

Once these kittens with fur grew up they were bred back to Sphynx cats. About one half of the kittens in their litters would be hairless. It took a long time to create the breed this way.

The Cat Fanciers' Association recognized the Sphynx as a breed in 1998. These cats are rare. Breeders have waiting lists for their kittens.

There are other hairless pets. Some breeds of dogs such as the Chinese crested lack fur. Hairless fancy rats are sometimes called the Sphynx rat.

People feel very strongly about Sphynx cats. They either like or dislike this breed's strange appearance. Many are charmed by the cat's odd looks. They treasure this rare cat.

Sphynx kittens sell for around $1,500.

A Wrinkled Alien

The Sphynx is a medium-sized cat. Males can weigh between 8 and 11 pounds (4 and 5 kg). Females are smaller. They weigh between 6 and 8 pounds (3 and 4 kg).

This breed is long and slender. It has strong muscles. The Sphynx has a round belly that makes it look like it just finished a huge meal! The chest is also round like a barrel. The cat's long tail comes to a point at the end.

Loose skin makes the Sphynx look wrinkled. All cats have wrinkles. But those on a Sphynx are easier to see since they have no fur.

The cat's face looks like an alien's. Its head is shaped like a wedge. Their giant ears look like they belong on a bat. Sphynx ears can be up to 3 inches (8 cm) tall. Sphynx cats also have huge eyes. They are shaped like lemons.

Both the body and head of a Sphynx cat are wrinkled.

Suede Coats

Sphynx cats are not truly hairless. They have **down** coats. The down feels like warm **suede**. Some cats grow puffs of fur on their toes and tails. Many do not have any whiskers.

Some cats grow extra down in the winter. Then they shed it in the spring. Others stay bald all through the year.

Sphynx cats come in many colors. The skin gives the Sphynx its color. The cat can be one solid color, such as red. Or it might be two colors, such as black and white. These colors look like they are tattooed onto the cat! A Sphynx cat's coloring stays the same for its whole life.

There are several patterns to choose from. **Calicos** have patches of three colors on their skin. **Tortoiseshell** mixes patches of red and black on their white skin. **Tabbies** can have stripes or spots.

Most Sphynx kittens are born with thick fur. This fur becomes thinner as they become adults.

Some Sphynx cats have a calico pattern on their skin.

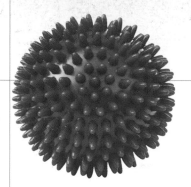

Lap Cats

Sphynx are very friendly cats. They have been called "lap cats" since they follow people around. Sometimes these cats wag their tails like dogs!

Sphynx cats like to hang out with people of all ages. They greet guests by giving them head butts. They make quick friends with other cats and most dogs.

Kittens and cats seek out warmth because of their lack of fur. Two of their favorite spots are on their owners' laps and in their beds. They huddle in front of heaters. They cuddle beside computers. They nap in sunny windows. Some people even dress their cats in warm clothes!

After naps these cats burst with energy. They swing from the tops of doorways. They jump high up onto bookcases. They open doors to search for bags of cat food. Sphynx can get into mischief. But it is hard to stay mad at them.

This breed has been described as "part monkey, part dog, part child, and part cat."

Sphynx cats enjoy snuggling under blankets and covers.

Famous Felines

Sphynx love to be in the limelight. They are born movie stars. With their odd looks they steal the scenes. These cats can grab an audience's attention! Plus they are one of the most easily trained cat breeds.

Mr. Bigglesworth appears in a series of Austin Powers movies. This Sphynx is popular with the adult audience who watch these action-comedy films. Dr. Evil is Mr. Bigglesworth's owner. Three kittens took turns playing the role of another cat named Mini Mr. Bigglesworth.

This breed also stars in TV shows. One Sphynx cat appeared in *Sabrina the Teenage Witch*. Sabrina told her cat Salem to get a new look. The cat took her advice. It turned into a Sphynx cat.

A character on the hit 1990s TV show *Friends* spent $1,000 on a Sphynx cat. She wanted a cat just like her grandmother had. One of her friends claimed the cat was "inside out."

Some Sphynx cats have earned roles in films, such as the Austin Powers series.

Cat Care

Sphynx can live 15 years or longer. Cats need to visit veterinarians. This helps to keep them healthy. Vets check the cats all over and then give them **vaccines**.

Cats should be kept indoors. This is the safest spot for them to live. Plus the sun is unsafe for Sphynx. They can get sunburned since they are not covered with fur.

Cat supplies help them feel at home. Cats need beds to take catnaps. They need crates for trips. They need bowls for food and water. And they need litter boxes where they can go to the bathroom.

Cats also need scratching posts. They quickly learn to sharpen their claws on posts.

Sphynx need weekly baths. They do not have fur to soak up body oils. So their skin gets oily. Their ears need to be cleaned often because they get waxy. And they need to have their nails trimmed too.

Some people give their Sphynx hot water bottles to cuddle with. They also buy them sweaters!

Scratching posts keep Sphynx from ruining furniture and carpets.

19

Showoffs

Sphynx are very smart. They can learn how to do tricks. Then they show off all of the tricks they have learned. They like to clown around. They enjoy being the center of attention.

These cats need many toys to keep from getting bored. They love puzzle toys to test their brains. They like to chase laser toys. They are drawn to toys that make sounds. They bat around toy mice. Balls are also a big hit.

Sphynx can use their toes as fingers! They will pick up toys using their front toes. This comes in handy when playing a game of fetch.

This breed enjoys company and does not like being alone. They like to play with other cats. This way they can amuse each other!

A top game is stealing people food. Sphynx like to snack on almost anything!

Toys with feathers will keep Sphynx cats busy and out of trouble.

Glossary

breed (BREED) A breed is a group of animals that are different from related members of its species. Sphynx cats are a rare breed.

calicos (KAL-i-kohz) Calicos are animals with blotched or spotted coats. Sphynx cats can have a calico coat.

down (DOUN) Down is a covering of something soft. Some Sphynx cats have down covering their bodies.

prey (PRAY) Prey is an animal hunted by another animal for food. Sphynx cats pounce on their prey.

suede (SWAYD) Suede is a soft leather that has been rubbed on one side to make the surface feel less coarse. The down on Sphynx cats feels like suede.

tabbies (TAB-ees) Tabbies are cats with striped or spotted coats. Sphynx cats can be tabbies.

tortoiseshell (TOR-tuhss-shel) Tortoiseshell is a pattern on a cat with black, cream, and red markings. Some Sphynx cats have tortoiseshell coats.

vaccines (vak-SEENS) Vaccines are shots that prevent animals or humans from getting an illness or disease. It is important for a cat to get a vaccine so it doesn't get sick.

To Learn More

BOOKS

Gagne, Tammy. *Amazing Cat Facts and Trivia*.
New York: Chartwell Books, Inc., 2011.

Owen, Ruth. *Sphynx*. New York:
Rosen Publishing, 2014.

WEB SITES

Visit our Web site for links about Sphynx cats:
www.childsworld.com/links

Note to Parents, Teachers, and Librarians: We routinely verify our Web links to make sure they are safe and active sites. So encourage your readers to check them out!

Index